*slow curve*

# *slow curve*

### *Jeanne-Marie de Moissac*

COTEAU BOOKS
WWW.COTEAUBOOKS.COM

Edited by Judith Krause.
Cover and book design by Duncan Campbell.
Cover image, "Crescent Moon," by Yoshinori Watabe / PHOTONICA.
Printed and bound in Canada at Gauvin Press.

Library and Archives Canada Cataloguing in Publication

De Moissac, Jeanne Marie, 1952-
Slow curve / Jeanne Marie de Moissac.

Poems.
ISBN 1-55050-302-2

I. Title.

PS8557.E48193S56 2004    C811'.54    C2004-904997-6


1  2  3  4  5  6  7  8  9  10

Available in Canada and the US from:
Fitzhenry & Whiteside

401-2206 Dewdney Ave.
Regina, Saskatchewan
Canada   S4R 1H3

195 Allstate Parkway
Markham, Ontario
Canada   L3R 4T8

The publisher gratefully acknowledges the financial assistance of the Saskatchewan Arts Board, the Canada Council for the Arts, the Government of Canada through the Book Publishing Industry Development Program (BPIDP), the Government of Saskatchewan, through the Cultural Industries Development Fund, and the City of Regina Arts Commission, for its publishing program.

  Canadä

*This book is for my children*
*Rachel and Jesse*

# Contents

## fire makes its own wind

## cold front moving in

# *wet with light*

*fire makes
its own wind*

*wind-spilled*

i.


tulip clothespinned to the line
yellow bow hung out to dry

dry spring

wind-dried, sun-dried
soil turned on its backside

raw, black muscle
worked to dust

potatoes in the dust
looking for eyes in the Yukon Gold

ring around the sun
what will it bring
what could it mean

how much blood must be spilled
to settle the dust
still the wind

ii.


swans in the summerfallow
drifts of white in the furrows

northern movement
last sign of winter

seems every sign has been shot at least once

yield – hard to know which way to turn
which signal to use
slow curve – the hand that follows it

squeeze left

you never know what you might find
when you leave the road

bound to be dirt
bound to be stones

underneath the melt
the stones have been moved
the prairie scraped away

yet the shape is still there
a slow recognition of self
wind-spilled

the unveiling
  alb and shawl
and unwrapping
  chasuble and cassock

reflection of my face in salt water
how one becomes two in recognition

how could the swans fit in this
always coming back
layers stripped away

some recognition of shape
some way to be in it

iii.


trick of the eye
grasses

like the trick the thistle plays
pretending to be a potato

how the grey cat at dusk
is a mound of dirt by the corn
so still she is in her affairs

how sometimes the grey and shimmer
of wolf willow becomes coyote

the stone, a fawn
tucked inside buckbrush

and the chokecherry
round and dark, solid against the storm

o buffalo

shapes move out of the rain
shift in the summerfallow

*necklace of dark moons*

i.


the sky is blue in the spring
bluer than anything, anything

and the grass is dry in the spring
any chance it will burn like gasoline

my daughter brings me three hanging baskets
filled with willow branches

hangs them in the garden
hangs them in the trees
one, two, three

truth is
when spring comes, I'm never quite ready

time to turn this cup of blood over to my daughter
with the flood of first woman tears
the sleeping time over abruptly as it began

run a bath
garnets and dark rubies swim around me

ii.

crows catch the tail of a spring storm home
unclasp this necklace of dark moons
put the dance in my belly

rock it
roll it

blood finds a way to become

the way fear finds comfort in my lonely bed
only warmth is my own creation

feelings tied to the flesh
finding a hot place to coagulate

iii.


snow twirling down too late
and lost as the wind

like I lost you
you are nowhere
my comfort the ache in the middle of my longing

fire catches – makes its own wind
stopped only by the long wash of salt

draw a line in the clay
wet poultice of dirt
things burning themselves out

not without a fuss
not without a mess

how can blame be laid
when nothing is left

I send myself up in signals of smoke

*a windy poem*


i.


ashes and raindrops coming at once
falling at the same speed

the dawn stirs the wind
and I think of him
his face against my wandering mouth

oh, Queen Bee
come and rescue me
seems I've fallen in love
with the sun

come, Queen Bee
I'm not one to beg

there she is, low

heavy with her purse of eggs

ii.


when I think of him
there's movement in my womb
geese pass under a setting moon
morning

how there is no doubt
two geese make a pair

o union

the need to touch each other
even in flight

o wind, o blow

you can't seem to make your mind up about anything these days

coaxed up by the grasses
in their need to brush against each other

iii.


April – snow falling over a setting moon
belly wool, drylicked soft

songbirds scold the snow, the cold
movement towards another

eat quick

so much to do
before he arrives

so many things to set straight
time is short
honey-sweet in the deliverance

falseness seems more apparent
in the bright of spring

long light shows all transparencies

*second-hand stones*

i.


quill pokes out of my daughter's arm
sharp as her words

she plucks it out – not ready for wings
or any of the new things she sprouts

but she's ready to take flight

choose your poison carefully
hide it hide it so no one sees

a premature ejaculation
there isn't time for niceties

my urgency filled with transplanting

after all, spring waits for no one
waits for nothing

blows in wind gusts and hope
to keep all grasses in their places
so they can't take back the garden

ii.


magpie feather greens up
  blues up
  turns up
underneath the second-hand stones my son
hand-picked from rock piles

hard as the stones beneath his skin
skin that changes texture
with each sprouting hair
things coming finally to their dead centre rest

turn the quern for your mother
she loves you like no other
grind the wheat and she will feed you

iii.


geese on their nightly stroll through the barley stubble

knowing only the music of what might be left
knowing only the earth's dance between light and shadow

*deliverance*

wide open eye
prairie sky winking down

baby's breath, full bloom

smells like every prairie girl
opened her mosquito-bitten thighs

opened them wide with a July full moon

nothing to hide
say the passersby on this busy road
windows open wide as the sky

after all, flowers wear sex
on their faces

nothing to hide
says the full bloom moon

no need for cover-up and foundation
no need to repent

the give and take of love
flows free, scent

*Gabriel*

poor Mary
stones gather
in the corner of your eyes

you uncover them
the way spring uncovers
secrets winter kept

heat – all curliness of hair, all brightness of wing as you call him in
    brush of veil against your skin

oh, Mary – how could you crave another

at least there is the comfort of his name
you roll it around on your body

what is your name
what is your name

he tastes of stone, you think

what is your name
what is your name

as he fills you
touches the end of you

he kisses his name into your mouth

*a mixing*


weeds have muscled up, thickened with the heat
dew the only water for miles

my roots have gone deep
trying to find their way to water, underneath the hardpan

rain
we'll call her Mary
we are without grace
and my fingers are stained with the picking

saskatoons, strawberries
sweet grass and raspberries
a mixing of juices

river – cool slit of wet in the hottest part of summer
people dragging their boats for miles across the hot land

heat forcing the heads, turning the seed
a purity that needs only water, only water
a light so thin and hot it shows the bones of everything

northern lights and lightning, a balance of cool and heat
I am caught between two train tracks   feet up
suspended between two lights

heart beating close to the surface of things
let me drench you

smoke finds its way south through the dark, the fog
a transference of light

a mixing of smoke and steam
finding a place we can be together

*petroglyph*

i.


endings and beginnings
are more predictable than middle ground
where walking is done
blessed by the earth as I bless it with my feet

here the grass is sweet
plump with spring water

here the grass is dry
thin enough to see its bones
and stones have stored all the day's heat

I feel it through my boots – hard to put them on
bare feet, o my feet

do I give shape to the land, to the stone
when I touch it with my feet, my hands
the way your hands give shape
to my breast, my bones

can the hawk scream the rain in

does my little girl stir the wind when she swings
she tells me it is so

here lies the middle ground

ii.

hills throw their shadow
and it settles, pelt of bear

covers Eagle Creek
thick hide tucks the water in

stillness – hoofprints
beaten into the stone

the wind speaks of the stillness
tells the coolness of the stone

shadow of my breast against the stone
long spine distorts the nipple

for a moment
I don't recognize my flesh

breath changed by what's been carved
a grace in the curve of ribs

a generosity of place
a place for everything

open arms, warm
as the hot sweet smell of saskatoons

last of the berries ready to pound
turned into shadows by the heat

follow the path
you made with your fingers

to the stillness of stones
movement inside stillness

*everything is for always*


some cliffs beg to be springboards
this garbage jumps onto buffalo bones

and she sits, on her haunches
peers across the coulee
guards the bones, guards the garbage

she breathes a veil of smoke
around her wind-shredded, grocery bag hair

I kneel before her
she smudges me with an exhale of her smoky breath

where shall I place my offering, goddess of the garbage
lady of the refuse

can you open your cloak wide enough
for all my mistakes

and she takes a buffalo shin bone
turned to stone

drums on a water heater
drums in the thunder

her long breasts sway
in the wind before the storm

and I dance till the rain comes in

*morning calls*

the way grasses call
for light upon the dew

the way night calls
water up from the ground

I walk out to her, barefoot

wash my face in the sages
in honour of the horses
and the careful way they awaken

the yarrow knows where she hides
where she curls to sleep behind the hills

a murder of crows knows too
they speak amongst themselves

how some days she's shy
to show her pretty face

*a gathering*


i.


don't forget the finch
and the stillness of the yellow

as she teaches the leaves
joy in the surrender

surrender in the fall
long passage down
down into the stillness

stillness of grasshoppers
the slow hot way they fuck
as if there's nothing better to do

rub me a little

I'll come away in pieces of stone

ii.

hollyhocks, and the bees who spiral into them

wrapped, drunk and slow
in a thick blanket of pollen

applesauce spirals to the left

and the crows are flocking
circle dancing

a gathering on gravel
parting for my truck like some black sea

murder in the barley
sacrifice of summer

they settle in the tops of dead cottonwood trees

bleached grey bones
alive for a moment
with dark leaves

iii.


I loosen my hair into the wind
into the stone circle

vantage point

belly button gathers information
first mouth
filters what comes in
my body an open place

the ladybugs gather
greedy for secrets

iv.

black cat finds shade underneath my skirt
hot September

not a cloud in the sky
a sure sign of rain, my mother would say

the air is still
I'm only aware of the cricket's song
when it has been silenced

my hair loses its curl
when you are gone

I will knit while I wait
with wool I have gathered

knit you a sweater of prairie wool

when it's finished
and I've sewn the pieces together

I'll embroider avens on each sleeve

bluebells at the throat
rose petals over the heart

and crickets, black
singing their song of love

all around the belly
all around the belly

v.

the tom comes home, hard
all lap kittenness
gone with his meow

static when I stroke him

smoke-filled clouds
tarot cards in the fallen leaves

the magician, changer of all seasons
lifts the green skirts of cottonwood trees

and what's this we see
bright yellow slip

sheer enough to see the shape of her limbs

the ladybugs gather in the last heat of summer
and the last of the crickets sing one long inhale

until the dance is exhausted
like your hand, lost in my green dress

*the pull*


i.


the separation between lawn and prairie
wood and lawn

where to stop cutting
how to determine the line

there must be some place
some junction

off go the petticoats
just like mother said

off come the layers
red and white and red

I paint my toenails yellow
canola blossoms
July afternoon

bright as the light you're wrapped in

ii.


the moth knows the separation between dark and light

moth, wrapped inside my house
moon, trapped outside my house

how long can he fly against the glass
beating away the invisible
with his wings

my dress, a hair shirt of spear grass

there, and there
small flies
proof of my skin
my nerves, the place I begin

blood dries in the breathless morning
water pulled towards the light

*cold front moving in*

*take me to the river*

i.


I thought it would be complete
with take-me-to-the-river gospel singers

I'd follow the floral wave of print dresses
down the steep bank

I thought these same women
would get naked in the river
ready to scrub me down

did I half expect to see Suzanne
waiting with a fresh pot of tea

her grandmother's babushka
filled with the last of the oranges

the water is winter lazy
bracken muddy brown

nothing has greened

is this where I spit the bitter pill
I've been holding in my mouth

oh, the water moves
make no mistake about it

but I am lost to it

ii.

I haven't a cup of sweet tea
to offer you, grandmother
in exchange for your kind words

though I see by the way you are perched
this tree meets your approval

I would whisper things to you, grandmother
though I only speak them into the wind

can you separate voice from air

my heart is a closed room
filled with unanswered letters

your smooth head is familiar
your sharp eyes see my milk has let down
round cups filled
will sour if I don't leak soon

she looks up
I follow her blue-black direction

a pair of hawks embrace in the arms of the wind

iii.


this wild old woman
calls the hilltop home

see the stone, large and flat
it is her table, her bed
it is the drum

don't be surprised if she hums about herself
or about the stone

she may be busy with her hair
it takes most of her time
such grave responsibility

when she binds it tightly, the air is still
when she loosens the knot, it becomes the wind

she licks the dew morning casts upon the stone
and waits, with the stone
for buds to green beneath the waxing moon

iv.

prairie wool sings – strong winds
lift last year's pale nurse grass
the green underneath, surfacing

my nipples are antennae
arriving ahead of the rest of me
assessing the situation

predicting light, dark
predicting rain

the winter was dry
just enough snow for one load of your laundry

now the only sound of rain
is the song dripping
from the meadowlark's beak

the river flows blood
I shall dab my points red

no sense waiting around
until the river flows milk

meantime, I've brewed a strong drink of tea
bitter enough to pucker the inside of your mouth

here, dip your spoon in the honey pot

I have only one cup
we will share

*red-willow wound*

i.


pain follows me
stained fingers

stray dog, I am the bone

or is it pleasure
they register together

sometimes the labour
goes on and on
no breaking sign

the blizzard breaks the tops of trees

and these bees I've held
all winter in my mouth, sticky sweet feet

(oh, they're no trouble – no one suspects)

well they add a certain resonance
to my voice
a certain sweetness
to my disposition

they awaken with the storm
want outside to stir the wind a little more

you're not alone, little girl

these last bees
reluctant to leave my sleepy mouth
are for underneath your tongue

apple blossoms for your throat
hold them for comfort
hold them for sweetness

while the last of the blizzard
is caught in the trees

echo of snow burns my face

ii.

don't let them see blood
they go crazy
chicken crazy

one taste and they can't get enough

must be the salt...

o dance, little daughter
spring is here

won't there be rivers to direct
cigarette butts to rake

dance till your heart stops aching

iii.

*for Cree and his spottiness*

the hills are wild ponies
pintos and paints
oh, ride, I say
ride

besides – in spite of best intentions
each time you come you pinch a little soul

it is I, little mole
must be spring

rustle around
wake up the ground

sluff of winter edges a slough

will the aspens be enough
promise of leaf

I can't hold them in my arms

sweet song
spring birds

woodpecker calls bugs from the trees
and the wind gallops the hills
stirs up the bees

iv.

the roots seem dark

careful whose ear receives
these things not meant for all to hear

a quick ritual
instant coffee, a blow job

but what three-legged beast
shall I give birth to this time

dawn, and the moment before
dusk, and the moment after

I am part of no audition

o wind

how to unlearn what father told you
how to let mother hold you

v.

winter has taken the fat
fire lights quickly

pattern of wind, wide and bright
as the smile of a woman who's been hit

o wheat

I set you on fire
grief's garden
white ash
worked into the clay

o temple of green

fire moves quickly
turn your back for a moment

the whole house burns down

vi.

kitty cats and crystal balls

sshh
careful comes
slow and heavy as spring wet snow

who will you pick for your first time, princess
what about tom up the road

son of Moses
and that Queen who slipped into the crowd
took the barn over
wintered in a milky pile of orphan lambs

the Queen without ears
who disappeared up the road

I believe he's called Tiger

clandestine meeting, full moon greeting

vii.

train calls through the coulee
echo, nobody's fooling
anyone any more

geese Vs don't worry about trains
not like they worry about summerfallow

exposed muscle
wearing down the last of the hump

at least that's what the magpie said
perched on a stop sign
black, white, and red

can they ever be quiet
can they leave anything unsaid

wind echoes in the cottonwood tree
finds first leaves of hollyhocks

who fool you, showing up
where you wouldn't expect anything to grow

a place for stones

stones need no explanation for their piling
they need no apology

viii.

I work best in the dark
I've been wandering there
calling your name

defined by how I brush against the air
where my hair meets creation

I gather myself

defined by wind, howls as it enters
and breath, howls as it leaves

I gather light
the way crows gather
beneath their wings, wind

a folding in

the way we turn in at the start
in at the finish

ix.


hiss of frankincense
hand upon my breast

let-down
rushing milk river

o river, milk river

here are my legs
branches of the willow
part them

here is my hair
grasses
here is my blood

here is where the willow
pulls blood up from the ground

red-willow wound

a place of light

x.

I've gathered the bones
left by winter, hot fire
cremation in the burning barrel
on the first dry night

black cat

songs, there if you call for them
waiting, like spring
like me

a candle in the window

and there you are in my crystal ball
looking back at me with your blind eye

I send my red willow tongue into the dark
seems the only thing to do

no rules

where's the fire, ask the witches
they seem to draw it to them

wet April, good time to weep
good time to sweep spells from the trees

back porch huddle
two witches and a nun
compare cauldrons to sugar bowls
beginnings to ends

xi.


wake up, Queen Bee
cat's paw in milky tea
sweet lick

I set bread for my beloved
round cheek on the small of my back

put it near the fire
his tongue finds the place I begin
the rise

punch down what has risen
shape each loaf with kisses

does my breast have shape
without your hand

are my lips sweet
without your mouth

I bake the bread
any second you might walk through the door
the house will smell of love

o slope of shoulders

if I put the kettle on
you'll be here by the time the tea has brewed

wind howling in a minor key
reflecting the pout, the sulk of the sky
temper, temper

cold front moving in from the arctic

xii.

I deliver myself
into your hands, half-formed

can you be gentle
now you've tasted blood

there are things we won't speak of

how the red of willow bleeds
itself into the green, the spring
the alkali smell where you begin

we won't speak of these things

not here

I only sought solace in your shoulders
buffalo slope
build for speed and endurance

fleece – a place to nest

May outside
she opens her thighs
wrings out the spring

*wet with light*

*peaches*

the swallows have gathered
while my garden sleeps under gold
wheat, ripe – burned by heat and grief

all colour drained into the heat
except the last few pinks of hollyhock

and the red geranium
tucked into the rose bush

loose bloom, pieces of a broken heart

I should really cut a slip
root it in rainwater

wait for a new heart to bloom

peaches on my counter, ripe for syrup
wait for jars, skins reluctant
to leave the meat, so difficult
to separate fruit from pit

I wrap myself around this last bit of light
smoke filled

thick as our kisses
thick as my nipple, spun in your mouth

*blood moon*

i.

*for Diane*

can raven and owl work together
or is their work best done
in secret from each other

where there will be no competition
where there will be no refusal

old cornstalks, bones
white in the full-moon light
keep time to the wind

touching each other
rustle and staccato
shakers and drums

humming in the garden

stage set
fire lit

here comes the bride
unescorted

she offers herself to the smoke
offers her dress to the fire

it burns red, a rising blood moon
then turns black
polyester heart

and now the bouquet
the left shoulder
toss it over

toss it through the veil
that trails behind
o milky way of tears

someone will be there to catch it

ii.


leave the clothes on the line past dark
and they choke with dew

the clothespins are darker than the dark
the line and these clothes
both darker than the night

surprising how the dark really isn't

a veil of shadows
black cats in layers

waxing moon wrapped in a scarf of clouds
against late October – the thought of dawn
the only thing that warms
though it's coldest at first light

how dark on dark is the blackest of shadows

there must be some counterpoint
before a moon shadow is levelled by the dawn
some silence between shadows

iii.

*for Rachel*

pentacle burning
ashes, a fallen star

star falling in the water
starfish

words are words

once said, the net is cast
the spell is set

my daughter, her breath
the comfort it gives me

last of the blood moon
rises at first light

cat scratch
bleeds into the dawn

iv.

*for Jesse*

the old moon
bent into herself
is weary

oh, sun
she whispers

have I not given birth to you
more times than even I remember
have I not suckled you
holy elixir

oh, sun
have I not encouraged your path

see how I am feeble
see how I cannot hold my own light

beloved mother, he hums
and lifts her in his arms
tucks her face, transparent
into his shoulder

*communion*

i.


the sacrament is open
sacred fluids have been spilled

this cup of light
once set upon the credence
is empty

turned over on the altar
the last few drops disappear into the cloth

will there be no communion
no matter – I fear this blister on my lip
would adhere to the dryness of bread without wine
of body without blood

besides, he burned my mouth with his tongue

how could I be the same
it's changed the way I breathe
the way I walk

ii.


he runs until the new moon has set
hides in the dark

the blood moon comes full
no place to run, no place left to hide
the spell inside his open mouth

meantime – the last of the crows fly south
with the first hard frost and the priest has run off
with some widow he plays golf with

some widow, rich with promise
wet with light

*blink*

flies are crazy in the morning
drawn to the light, the heat

life and death in a blink
on my windowsill

harvest of everything ready at once

a shame to waste the apples
but there's not enough time for all the addictions

fly swatter
fly slaughter
bug butcher says my daughter

swat the flies on my thighs
on my grandmother's afghan
still hot, years later, with her stitches

in the kitchen the flies are thick
heavy as the house when the son is gone

heart of salt
a dry bleed

no one's at fault

blink and he's a man

oh, how time flies
how time tricks you
into believing the days are long

the apples have fallen for you
bursting with pink and sun
waiting to be turned into wine by the prairie
a compost of everything

a hanging on in spite of the wind
in spite of the whine and moan of the train

click clack
click clack

pain of the track stirs the ground for miles

the mourning dove hears
she moans for you

morning, stillness
the wind hasn't chosen a direction

and something needs to be done
with all the tomatoes
the bones the dogs leave everywhere

the bloody rags

*stir the fire*

glass shatters on impact
won't withstand the pressure

pressure under seal

sealers and recipes
secrets in jars

canners passed from witch to witch
fire to fire

coming to a head
a long slow boil

stir it down, stir it down,
on the double

gather the pumpkins it looks like snow, says my daughter

snow on the cosmos
before they've bloomed

doomed like the rags I leave behind

blood and grease
an invitation open-ended
to participate in the bleed

a bed to seed what might be coming next

what might happen when I've sifted through the ashes
when the jars have been filled

will I be the one to hold the head of the wounded man
heat is food when you come face to face with yourself

the house freezes into place

stir the fire, stir it up
ashes in my hair

*cold*

slips into the extremities

at first I don't notice
then I pretend
I don't notice

my arms lose feeling
and I know I'm still walking
because I see one foot, then the other

but there is no connection
to this snowy earth
three dimensions in white

there is no bite

if only the cold would do my bidding
I would try to catch up to my heartbeat

if only you would beat your drum for me to dance

could I dance fast enough
would you drum hard enough
to close the mouth of winter

the heart freezes last

*manicure*

i.


retracing the steps
going back further than I have memory

pushing back the cuticles
to hasten his arrival

no sweetness in such waiting

the cold is bitter
even nails well attended
crack against such weather

ii.

light seeps in through a crack
in my heel

cold snap
spring well-wrapped

a cold blanket folded and crumpled around the hills
no place to get warm

keeping vigil

married men in their state of grace
a place for everything

no heroes without war

I dress for battle
each time I walk through my front door

winter's front line

iii.


going out on the weekend to laugh
enough unfamiliar bodies to brush up against
to last the whole week

petit mort

rapture, the colour it invokes
  homage

winter's candle blown out by the first spring wind

cracks heal when the body
collects enough light

*wolf woman*

old woman walks the tracks
her silver hair rimed white
floats around her
moon bright, her only cloak

breath of fog
song of mist

she hums a small tune
a small wolfy tune for company

old woman holds a skull
before her   wolf
it is her eyes

she gathers the moon
mirrored in the icy hilltops
gathers the moon into the skull, blue light

as she walks the tracks

you hear her when the snowy world
turns blue with a full moon

the high note at the edge of the wolf's howl

*coyote in Hollywood*

*for Randy Taylor*


i.

coyote stands by the railway tracks
paw prints in the snow follow him
wherever he goes

he waits, howls for the whistle
waits for the engineer's lunch

I move through the zones and strip

no slow removal of clothes
in this change of season

quick acceptance of the skin

ii.


I gravitate to the ocean
pulls me like alkali
salty beginnings

beggar by the bus stop
Santa Monica and LaBrea

coyote in his feet

dares me to look
warns me not to

I wish for him
a warm place to sleep

somewhere between
concrete and water

o sing, coyote
sing

*a sled full of dog*


bridegroom, white
wrapped in a blue wedding sheet

stained shroud

a sled full of dog
dead, dead, dead
a toboggan full of stink

descent into the underworld is slowed
by rose bouquets
a thorny sled-blockade

and barbed wire catches in the sheet
tangles in his feet
his poor dear feet

the way is uphill till the end
salt-spill

nothing comes easy on too little sleep
love, a gentler sport come morning

farewell, bridegroom

I offer you to the land of the dead
magpies await

the empty sled a heavy weight behind me

coyotes break their burnt-toast fast
chant in the middle of the afternoon

*the walker*


the wind has almost died
and the moon rises on the other side of the storm

snow everywhere you were

filling in the spaces of your absence
blowing in the holes you left behind

yesterday's footprints have disappeared
no trace of the walker

I braid a veil of hair
to shield my eyes from the sun
when he comes
boom boom
to the beat of the solstice drum

dark moon in a dark time

the wood is wet
hisses as it burns
as it turns into heat

I will dab honey on the wound
wait for the light to quicken

*slow curve*

i.


winter comes, I sit inside it
as a seed is inside the winter of itself

hard shell a barrier between cold and life
exposed to the breath

walker, I call with my night eyes

if I wrap myself in the clothes of the father
the brother and the son
will they keep me from the cold
the snow and the wind

sinned against, I become the sinner

hard to make things fair
not by squaring everything that wants to curve

this path is not straight
it winds like a correction line
making amends

hard to see without wings how the land isn't square
how things don't make sense

the aspen bluff knows this
arcing itself in sympathy with the hills

ii.

this cradle gives little support
to the curve of my spine, my head

but walker, if you find me
you are welcome in my bed

though I suspect it's me
who is the seeker without sight

I hear you in my boots against the snow
feel you in the rhythm of my step
but there is no sight
only winter, only night

*mirage*


concentration of breath
in point form

fire – the spell is set
be careful what you ask for

red heart of wax clings to the rosy quartz
red samphire in a salty brine

seems pink where red meets white
pink where day meets night
where heat meets water

hard to surrender to beauty
to stop kicking the dead cow

the night shivers – I warm it
with the comfort my feet have
in each other

feeling luck in the mirage and herds
who single file from the bush at first light

*glass doors*

*for Anne Szumigalski*

winter come upon me
come upon me winter

lay your heaviness
alongside my body, my longing

grows as the day wanes

new moon, silver bit of longing

glass doors closed against
a song of spring

meadowlark singing
a February dream

\* \* \*

we sit close enough to be wrapped
in each other's scent

"it's alright to be afraid," she whispers
to the baby blue
baby Furby in her lap

they blink their owl eyes at each other

"the fearless are always afraid"

*witch flies south*

wraps the world in her moist breath

turns the sun silver
pale disc
a moon of fog

grasses, blond and auburn
compare frosted new 'dos

she wraps her cloak around her
travels in secret

whispers to the shadow of the hills
hears the moaning aspens, a prairie whine

listens discreetly to tales a river tells
gossip of the great wet slit

she paints her mouth red for the trip
only bit of colour in all this white

*winter train*

i.


devil spray-painted on a boxcar
waits to change tracks
waits for the switch to be pulled
hiss – the right of way

he keeps an eye on things
the whole length of the track

prairie is prairie is prairie

calls interference when he sees fit
makes no excuse for his constant erection

graffiti – the watch is in the movement of the train
low blow catches itself in the shadow between hills

white dogs, flanked
listen in the stillness for the death rattle
last leaves against the cottonwood tree

the hangers-on

while the sun hangs in balance with the moon
eyes to watch over the dead garden

ii.


blood and bone
water and stone

leave some things for the dark moon to figure out

I'm running on vapours

prairie is prairie is prairie

yet the shadow of my breath
against dead grasses fills me completely

as you filled me completely
the sky is bright as the moon is dark
brings up the moans

blood and bones
water and stones

iii.


stopping up the breath
changing the shape of things

holding the egg inside my hand
as if I owned it

as the filly owns the new moon

winter creeps in at night
the light changes

opens places summer kept secret
gets to the heart of things
while the train keeps track of time

prairie is prairie is prairie

the frost cannot be shaken
I feel no vibrations beneath my feet

time to cut away the callous
so the winter boot will fit

listen, buffalo
thunder down the track
bellow, older in the cold

*stone baby*

i.

I put my hands to bed
tuck them in around me
nails pink, lemon juice bath

will they still be dark come morning

I must scratch in the dirt
scratch at the dark
root in the aspen's rotting leaves

and the moss, oh yes, will be green come spring

with the first geese, the pussy willows

perhaps in the night
I dip my fingers into my own pussy

the water, hard now without the salt
stains my fingers

hard with bones of buck
bones of doe and stones that set the water table
with their beginnings

sediment settles in my womb
folding like breath of wind upon the snow

I am silent
while the stone, layer by layer
becomes itself

yet I scream in birth, hard water breaks

ii.

my stone baby has been delivered
lips, milky blue

won't have to rock this one to sleep
I'll hold her between my breasts

she will cool my hot body

I see you from the other side of the mirror
and my brush, my scissors – there

keep this safe for my daughter
it's a lock of my hair

*Acknowledgements*

Some of these poems appeared in *Grain Magazine, Poetry Wales, Amethyst Review,* and *We'Moon Date Book 2000, 2004.* "Take me to the river" was heard on CBC's Gallery.

I would like to thank Anne Szumigalski's poets and Elizabeth Brewster's poets for their sharp ears, my editor Judith Krause for her careful eye, and all the people at Coteau Books for their ongoing support. Finally, I would like to thank my children, Jesse and Rachel, for their love and for the life we've made together.

*about the author*

*Jeanne Marie de Moissac* is a prolific poet and short fiction writer. Her works have appeared in *Grain Magazine, Dandelion, Arc, Fiddlehead,* and even *Playgirl.* She has had her work broadcast on CBC Radio. Her first book, *Second Skin,* was published by Coteau in 1998.

Jeanne Marie was born and raised near Biggar, Saskatchewan, and currently lives on a farm in the Bear Hills near that town. She has spent many years working with Anne Szumigalski's and Elizabeth Brewster's poetry groups.